# The Great Gumshoe:
## The Case of the Missing Bear

by Amanda Litz

illustrated by
Christy Beckwith

Traveler's Trunk Publishing
Cedar Springs, Michigan

*This book is dedicated to my mom, who shared with me her love for the classic beauty and simple story telling of the black and white film era which inspired this book.- A.L.*

ISBN 978-0-9841496-4-3

CPSIA facility code: BP 313627

www.travelerstrunkpublishing.com

Printed in the United States of America

I'll never forget the day she walked into my life. The sun was hot, so I'd stopped by the soda shop for a tall glass of root beer. I was sitting on a stool reading the latest *Batman* comic. He was just about to catch the Joker when I looked up and saw her standing there.

The sun shone on her golden curls. She had two pink bows in her hair and she wore a matching pink dress. She was the prettiest dame I'd ever seen.

She looked at me with tears in her eyes. "Are you the Great Gumshoe?" she asked.

4

I jumped up from my stool, leaving the Joker's fate for another time. "That's me. How can I help you?" I replied.

"I've lost my best friend," she said, sobbing.

"Tell me about him," I said as I pulled a notepad and pencil from my pocket.

"Well, he's dark brown with brown eyes and a brown snout, and he wears a red shirt," she replied. "Hmm ... a brown snout." I said. "Is your friend a bear?"

"Yes. How did you know?" Her voice was full of hope.

"Just a hunch," I said with a smile. She wiped the tears from her eyes. "Can you please help me find him?" she begged.

How could I say no to a dame like that? I knew I had to find her bear. "What's your name, doll face?"

"Charlotte," she replied.

"All right, Charlotte. I'll find your friend," I said.

"Oh, thank you, Great Gumshoe," she said, and she kissed my cheek.

I cleared my throat. "Tell me what you did today."

"First Sally Mae came to my house for a tea party."

"Then I went to the park and the candy store."

"I was going to buy two grape suckers for Teddy and me. That's when I noticed he was gone!"

"Don't worry, doll. We'll find him."
I grabbed my hat from the counter,
and left some coins for the root
beer. "Follow me."

We had to retrace her steps to find the bear, so first we went to the candy store. We looked on all the shelves to see if she had set him down.

I pulled my magnifying glass out of my pocket to search for clues, but we didn't find any in the candy store not even a teddy bear hair!

Next we went to the park.

We checked the swings. No bear there.

We checked the slide. No bear there.

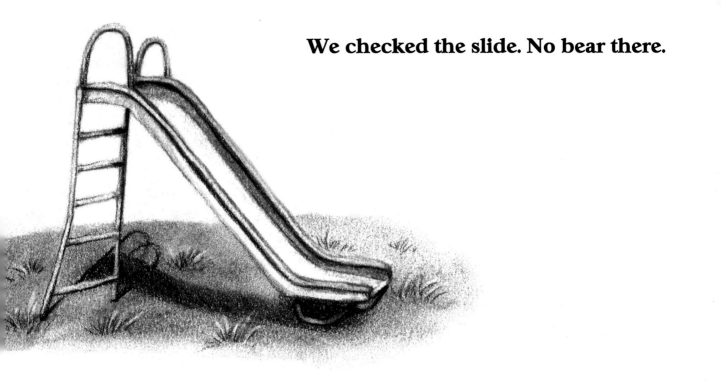

We even checked the merry-go-round. No bear there, either.

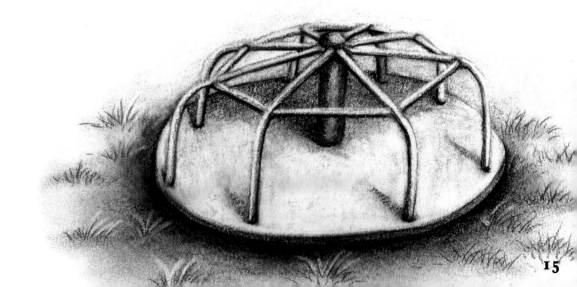

We walked back to her house.
She showed me her room.
"Is this where you had the tea
party?" I carefully looked around
the room for evidence.

"Yes, Sally Mae and I sat right over
there with Teddy." She pointed to
a round pink table.

I walked over to inspect it. It was set with three plates and three cups. There were cookies on two of the plates, and the third one had a fish. Teddy had been here.

I looked around the room for more clues.
A little red shirt was lying on the bed. I
walked over and picked it up.
"Is this Teddy's shirt?" I asked.

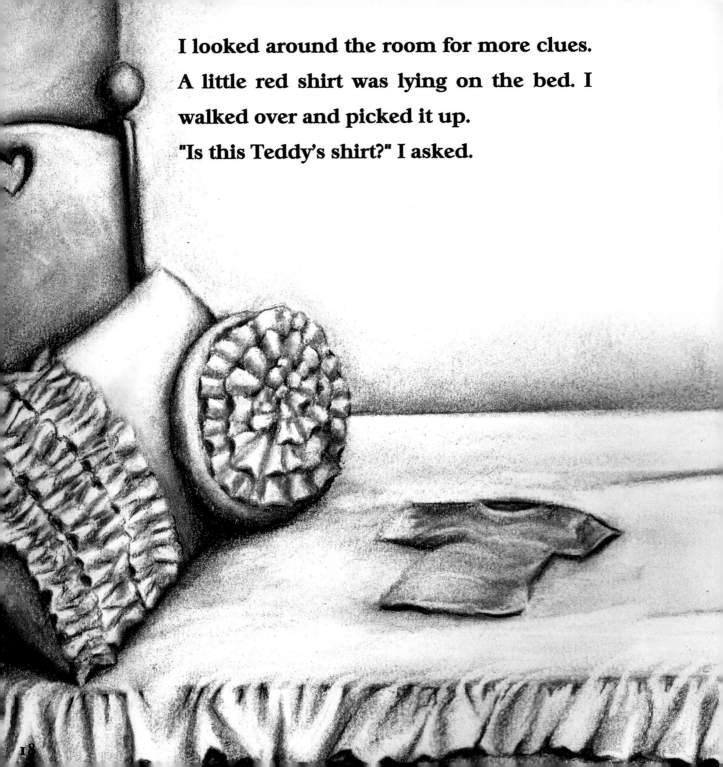

She grabbed the shirt from my hands. "Yes, this is his! I took his shirt off so we could go swimming."

We ran out to the pool to see if Teddy
was there.

"When you went swimming did you take
Teddy in the pool with you?" I asked.

"Yes," she replied. "Teddy loves to swim."

We looked in the pool and all around. There was no bear to be found. I didn't know what to do. We were at a dead end. We had looked everywhere and Teddy was still missing.

I had to think, so I sat down in a chair. I thought about the candy store, and the park, and the tea party in her room. There were no clues to tell us where Teddy might be.

Slowly, the seat of my pants started to feel wet. That was strange. Was it a clue? I looked down and saw that I was sitting on a towel. The towel was wet and kind of lumpy. Could it be?

23

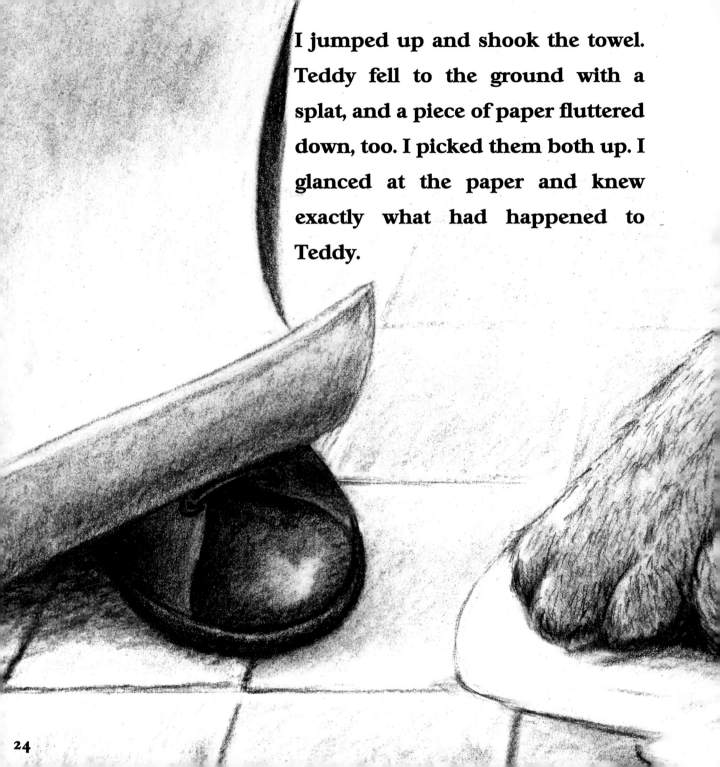

I jumped up and shook the towel. Teddy fell to the ground with a splat, and a piece of paper fluttered down, too. I picked them both up. I glanced at the paper and knew exactly what had happened to Teddy.

"You must have set him on the chair to dry and your mother covered him with a towel."

"How do you know it was my mother?" she asked.

"It's simple, really. This is a note," I said holding it up for her to see.

Dear Charlotte,
Teddy looked a little wet and cold so I wrapped him in a towel to make him warm and dry. Don't forget to bring him inside.
Love
Mom

She took Teddy and hugged him close. "I missed you so much!" She kissed the bear square on the nose. Then she looked at me with tears of joy. "Thank you for finding my bear. You are a very good gumshoe!"

"No, Charlotte, I am the Great Gumshoe,"
I said with a wink and a tilt of my hat.
Another case solved by the Great
Gumshoe! It was
time to go.

I was on my way back to the soda shop to see if Batman had caught the Joker, when she stopped me. "Wait!" she called. "Why do they call you Gumshoe?"

I glanced back, smiled and lifted my right shoe in the air. When she saw the bottom, she giggled. A giant wad of purple bubblegum was stuck to the heel of my shoe.

The End